# SAVVY CYBER KIDS
## AT HOME

### Adventures Beyond the Screen

Written by Ben Halpert
Illustrated by Taylor Southerland

Text copyright ©2014 Ben Halpert
Illustrations copyright © 2014 Savvy Cyber Kids, Inc.
Hardcover ISBN-13: 978-0-9827968-1-8
Paperback ISBN-13: 978-1-5005485-8-2
Library of Congress Control Number (LCCN): 2014912764
Published by: Savvy Cyber Kids, Inc., Atlanta, GA

To the children of the world, may you find balance in all aspects of your life.

To my friends and family, thank you for your continued support of Savvy Cyber Kids.

—Ben Halpert

:)

—Taylor Southerland

"OK mom, our 30 minutes of computer game time is up and we are bored.

Can we please get back online and continue the games we have explored?" asked CyberThunder.

CyberPrincess added,
"We don't know what to do.

The time we
were playing online
just flew."

Mom suggested, "CyberThunder and CyberPrincess, let's go make a list of things to do.

No! Wait! Let's make two!"

Mom continued, "One list for activities and games we can do inside.

And one list for activities and games we can do outside."

"Is that because on some days it's rainy?

And on other days it is sunny?" asked Tony.

Emma ran over with a pencil and paper and asked,
"Where should we start?"

Mom said, "We can write a list of things
that come from the heart."

"Some activities and games
are good for doing indoors;
while some activities and games
are good for doing outdoors.
And some are good for either.

It is so great you both are so eager!"
exclaimed mom.

Tony continued, "Or in a quiet corner of our home?"

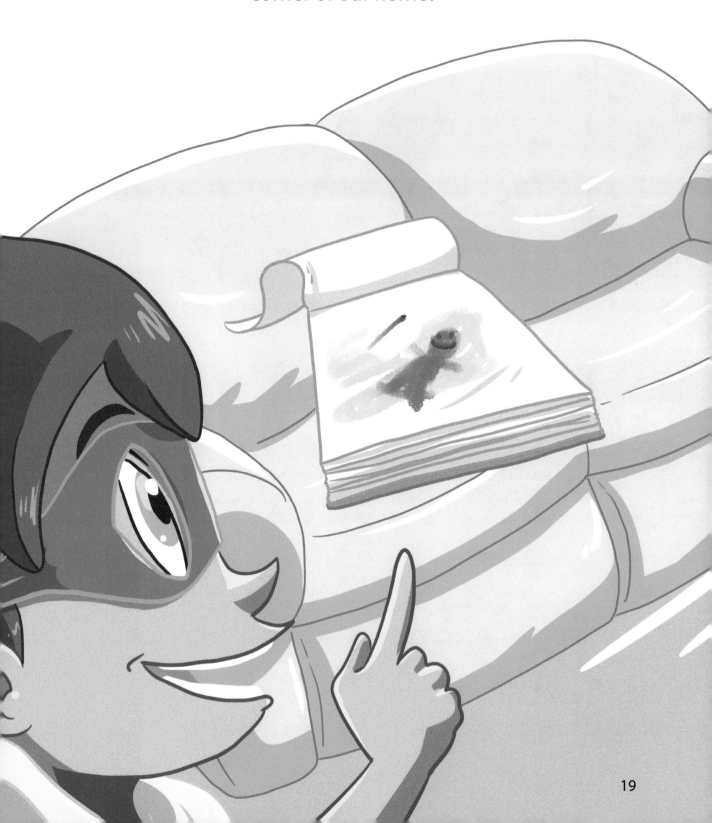

"You most certainly may.

Reading books are a great activity any day," mom responded.

"Once you start reading a book,

CATS?
CATS?
CATS.

YES, CATS.

you will most certainly get hooked."

Tony added, "You can learn how old the oldest person is in the world or which athlete is the fastest runner, along with other amazing facts."

24

Emma questioned, "You mean like the old machine you have in your office?"
"No sweetie, that is a fax," giggled mom.

"Great start kids, so we have 'explore books' on both lists.

How about a sport that doesn't involve using your fists?"

"Mom," said Tony, "what about the exercise where you go like this when you are wearing your exercise shorts?"

Emma shouted, "I love, Yoda!"
Tony laughed at Emma
and corrected her,
"Yoda is from Star Wars;
Yoga is one of many sports!"

Mom said, "Yes, Emma, great idea, we can spend some time singing!"

Tony added, "Then we can show how awesome we are at dancing!"

Tony shared another idea,
"We can go outside and
throw or kick a ball."

"And play around with all the pretty leaves if it is in the fall," added Emma.

"Mom," said Emma, "I have an idea for an activity for a rainy day.

We can donate
some toys to less
fortunate children
so they can play."

Tony added, "We can organize
our rooms and pick some toys.

We can donate them to
other girls and boys."

Tony said excitedly,
"And with paper, pencil, and
crayons we can draw pictures,
write a story or a letter.

Which would be great to send someone who is sick so they can feel better."

Mom added, "If the weather is nice outside, we can go to a nearby park."

"We can climb, swing, run, hide, and slide all day long until it gets dark," Tony said excitedly.

Mom said, "I knew you kids would not be bored if you were not online.

You can always use your imagination and play many games and activities rain or shine."

Mom, Tony shouted excitedly, "We can plan a 'Movie Night' for tonight where we can create our own movie tickets, cook our own popcorn, and make other tasty treats."

"Yeah!" said Emma, "That will be great
since we will have played outside all day,
so we can rest our tired feet!"

Mom said, "What a great list.

It seems there is nothing we have missed!"

Emma and Tony shouted: "Let's play the Savvy Cyber Kids way.

48

Always safe and protected online and offline every day!"

Download free activity sheets and a lesson plan at
www.savvycyberkids.org

## About Savvy Cyber Kids

The mission of Savvy Cyber Kids, a 501(c)(3) nonprofit organization, is to enable youth to be empowered with technology by providing age appropriate resources and education. Savvy Cyber Kids focuses on ingraining security awareness and ethics into the minds of children ages 3 – 7. Targeting children at the earliest of ages will enable appropriate decision making to be second nature as the child matures surrounded by a world filled with interactive technology.

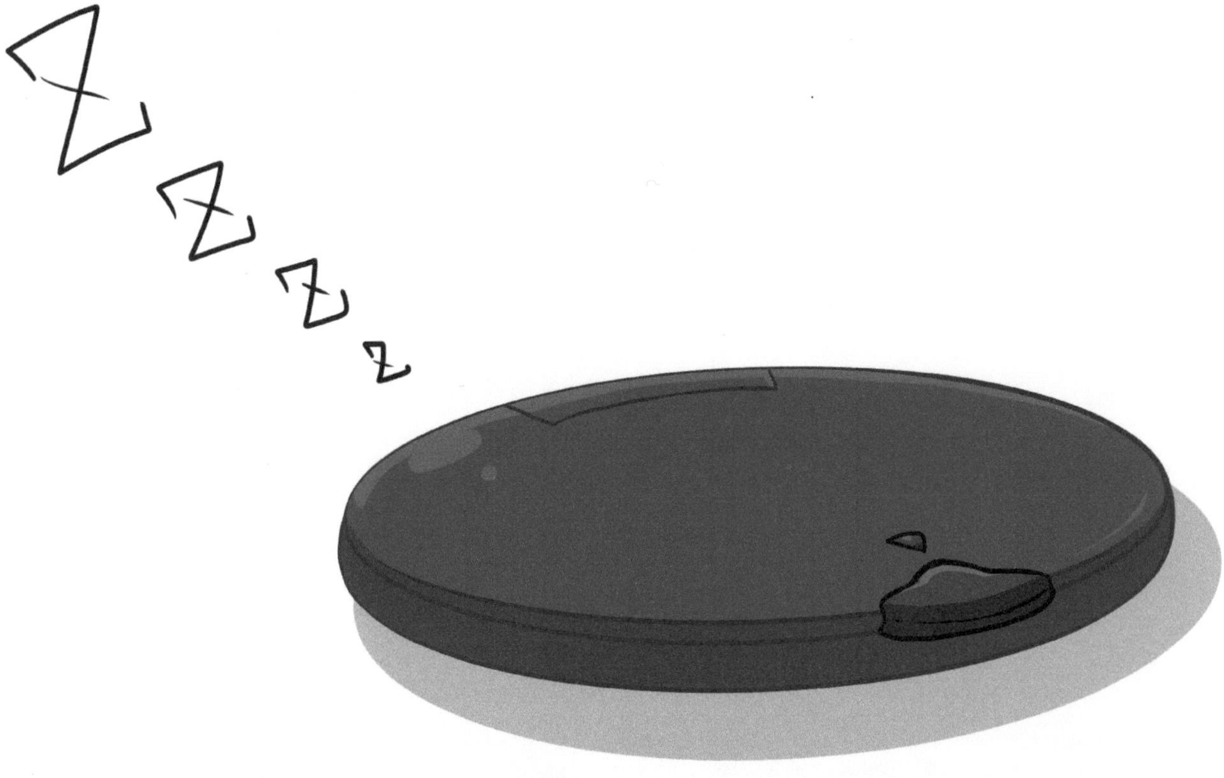
Z Z Z z

CPSIA information can be obtained
at www.ICGtesting.com
Printed in the USA
LVHW070402290720
661814LV00012B/584